What
Is
Right?

Veronica Lane Books

What Is Right?

By Etan Boritzer   Illustrated by Graham Sale

Third Printing 2009

Veronica Lane Books

www.veronicalanebooks.com   email: books@veronicalanebooks.com
2554 Lincoln Blvd. Ste 142, Los Angeles, CA 90291 USA
Tel/Fax: +1 (800) 651-1001 / Intl: +1 (310) 745-0162

Library of Congress Cataloging-In-Publication Data
        Boritzer, Etan, 1950-
        What Is Right?

Library of Congress Catalog Card Number 2004116828

SUMMARY: Various views and questions on ethics, integrity and fairness in social situations are presented for juveniltes to consider.

ISBN 9780976274315 (Hardbound) ISBN 9780976274308 (Paperback)

1. Ethics - Moral Decision Making - 170.20 Juvenile Literature
2. Children - Conduct of Lie, Juvenile Literature
    I. Sale, Graham, 1964-

...to the children of the world...

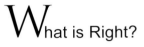
What is Right?

If you and your friend
walk down the street
on a hot, sunny day
and you see an orange tree
with lots of big, juicy oranges
growing in your neighbor's yard,
and some of the oranges
are hanging over the fence
into the street,
is it right to take a few oranges
for yourself?

Well, there are a lot of oranges,
and it *is* a hot, sunny day
and there is nobody else around—
so, is it right to take a few oranges
for yourself,
or not?

What is Right?

Grown-ups have a lot of rules
(sometimes grown-up rules are called laws)
and these rules are supposed
to tell us what is right
and what is not right.

But how do grown-ups
come up with all these rules?
Where did the first rule come from?
And anyway, what is the first rule?

Where did your Mom or Dad
or your teachers
learn what is right?
And do your Mom or Dad or teachers
always know and do what is right?

How can we ever know
the answer to this big, big question:
What is Right?

Maybe you and your brother
are supposed to pick up leaves
for your neighbor.

Suppose your neighbor promised
to pay one dollar to each of you
for picking up leaves
in his yard.

But what if your brother
works less than you do?
Should he still get a dollar?
Should he get less?

And should you tell your neighbor?
Or should you just talk it over
with your brother?

What is Right?

Sometimes we are not sure
what is right
and what is not right.

There are some things
that we *know* are not right—
and almost everybody knows
that these things are not right.

It is not right to steal.
It is not right to lie.
It is not right to kill
(or to hurt anyone).

But what if we do something
that maybe is not right
but is not something
like stealing, or lying, or killing?

What if we don't know all the rules?
What should we do if we are not sure
if something is right
or not right?

What if we only want
one or two oranges
out of that whole big tree of oranges-
is that really stealing?

What if we don't work
as hard as our sister
at picking up leaves?
It was only for a little while that
we didn't work as hard—
is that really lying,
to not tell our neighbor?

What if we want to eat some meat
and somebody has to kill an animal
for us to eat meat—
is that really killing?

How can we be sure
that we know
what is right
and what is not right?

Sometimes if we don't know
what is right, or are not sure,
we can try to find and listen
to a little voice somewhere inside us
called our *conscience.*

Now, nobody really knows
where this little voice
called our conscience comes from,
but sometimes people call it
the *voice of the heart.*

Nobody knows if animals
like dogs or cats,
or even fish or trees or bugs,
have this little voice inside them
or if only people have a conscience.

And nobody knows how this little voice
called our conscience
really even knows what is right.

But maybe if you don't know
what is right, or are not sure,
you can sit somewhere kind of quiet
and try to hear that little voice inside yourself
(maybe in your heart?)
and listen to what that voice is telling you.

But *how* does your conscience know
what is right?

Maybe your conscience can see
the whole big picture
of what you are doing
and what will happen,
or what you'll feel like,
after you do it.

Maybe we don't always see
the whole big picture
of what we are doing.

Maybe we only see
that big, juicy orange on a hot day.

But maybe our conscience
can help us to see
that big, juicy orange
doesn't really belong to us,
and maybe we shouldn't take it
without asking—
even if we think the person
who owns the orange tree
might not mind.

Sometimes we think we know
what is right,
but maybe we really don't.

Maybe it's your birthday
and you have a big party
and a BIG birthday cake
with lots of ice cream
and colored letters
and all kinds of stuff
all over it!

Maybe you think
that because it's *your* birthday
you should have the first
and biggest slice of cake
of any of your friends
at your party.

Is that really right?
Maybe what is right
is giving something
to somebody else
before taking for ourselves—
even if it is our birthday.

Sometimes we do something
that is not right
to try and make something else right.
Is that right?

Maybe a kid in class
is whispering
or bothering other kids in class
and making it hard
for them to pay attention
and learn.

And maybe the teacher
doesn't know about it.

So maybe some of the kids get angry
and want to hurt this noisy kid
after school.

But maybe this kid
has some problems at home
or has some special needs
and maybe we have to figure out
something better
than just getting angry at him
and doing what is not right

Some people say that what is right
is always right—
right in the beginning,
right in the middle,
and right at the end.

What does that mean?

If you know that it is not right
to hurt anyone
but those kids in class
hurt that noisy kid after school,
can that be right?

Maybe that kid
stops whispering in class
and bothering other kids,
after those kids hurt him.

But maybe that's because
that kid never comes back to school
after those kids hurt him.
Is that right?

Maybe if it is not right to hurt anyone,
that means you should never hurt anyone—
not in the beginning,
not in the middle,
and not at the end!

Does that sound like a hard thing to do?

Sometimes doing what is right
can be scary.

Maybe you want to tell those kids
after school
that it is not right to hurt
that noisy kid.
Or maybe you want to tell
a grown-up about it.

That's how doing what is right
can sometimes be scary—
because maybe those kids won't like you
if you try to stop them
from doing what is not right.

But does that mean
we should not do what is right,
because it is scary?

Maybe if we do what is right,
even if it is scary,
things will turn out all right,
do you think?

Can you teach a robot
what is right?

Suppose we teach a robot
what is right on our planet
and we send the robot
to another planet on a spaceship
to teach people on that planet
what is right.

Maybe the people of the other planet
will not think that what is right
on our planet
is right for their planet!

And maybe what is right
on their planet
will not be right for us either!

Maybe what is right for us,
is not right for our neighbor.
Maybe what is right for us,
is not right for other people
or not right in other places.

Can what is right
be different for different people?

How can we figure *that* one out?

Can two different things be right?

Maybe two people get into a fight
and each of them thinks he or she is right.

Sometimes when grown-ups get into big fights
they go to a place called *court*
and meet a person called a *judge.*
There they have to explain to the judge
what each of them thinks is right
(and sometimes they even shout
and it's really… not very nice).

Then the judge decides who,
and what is right,
and both people then have to do
what the judge says.
Do you think that is right?

Is it better for two people
to fight in front of a judge
or to fight when they are alone?

(Sometimes big groups of grown-ups
get really angry and have really big fights,
and sometimes they even kill each other—
and that's called war!)

How can we help
two different people,
or two different groups of people
both be right—
so that nobody gets hurt?

Can something feel not right
but somehow still be right?

Maybe one night there is a big storm
with lots of thunder and lightning.
(You're not scared, are you?)

And maybe, because of the lightning,
a tree in the forest catches on fire
and soon a lot of trees are on fire!
In the morning, the forest is all smoky
and a lot of trees are black and burned down.

Maybe we feel sad
about all the trees that burned down.
But sometimes things just happen,
happy or sad, right or not right,
and that's just called nature.

Fire is just a part of nature—
like lightning and thunder
and rain and sunshine
and grasshoppers and snakes
(and man-eating crocodiles)
and a full moon and clouds
and lady bugs and bees
and lots of other stuff like that,
are all part of nature.

So, can we really say
that something like a fire in nature
is right or not right?

How can something
that feels not right,
still be right?

How can what is right
be right for everybody?

How can what is right
always be right?

How can you, or anybody,
ever know what is right—
always and for everybody?

Do you know anybody
who knows
what is right
always and for everybody—
and for sure?

Have you ever heard
of anybody like that?

Have you?

What is Right?

Maybe What is Right? is a question
that we need to keep asking and talking about
with other kids and grown-ups every day—
maybe even forever.

Maybe sometimes we can even go
somewhere very quiet
and ask ourselves, very quietly
What is Right?

Maybe if we can hear
that *voice of the heart*
inside ourselves
and figure out What is Right?,
maybe we can start to feel really good inside
and maybe even kind of quiet
and nice inside.

But if we don't keep asking ourselves
What is Right?
and talking about it
with other kids and grown-ups
(maybe even with animals or trees or bugs!)
then we may *never* figure out the answer.

So, please, never stop asking
that big, big question:
What is Right?